MILK & HONEY

A COLLECTION OF SHORTS

D. ROSE

JR, my angel.
Nine years ago, you were taken away from us. Not a day goes by that I don't think about you. You're always in my heart.

CONTENTS

Hey!

This has been a project that I've wanted to do for a while. Writing a story in a limited amount of words really pushed me as a writer. And I am grateful for this experience

I hope you enjoy these **short stories** as much as I enjoyed writing them

~D.

MILK & HONEY

CAFFE MOCHA

1

MOCHA

*V*alentine's Day was my favorite holiday. Growing up, my parents made a big deal out of it. My dad had been my Valentine for as long as I could remember. He took my mom and I to dinner and gave us gifts. The older I get, the more I fell in love with the holiday. Since I moved away to school, my parents sent my gifts in the mail.

Oh, how I missed going to dinner with and opening a card with the sweetest handwritten message from them. This morning, they sent me a bouquet and an edible arrangement. I didn't get a chance to eat as much as I wanted because of class and then work. And The hopeless romantic in me loved watching others express their love for one another. Spending my favorite holiday at work watching couples make love connections beat staying home and watching a rom-com.

I watched as Kylan, the manager at Milk & Honey,

counted the drawer for the second time. Then, he disappeared into the back and returned with his jacket.

"You're leaving?" I asked, slightly disappointed.

Kylan was more than just my boss. He'd become more like a brother over the years since. I enjoyed working for Kylan because he was a team player. No one worked harder than him and he treated the team with respect. I also loved his advice. He was six years older than me but was wise beyond his years. No matter the topic, he knew what to say to get me back on track. Just this week, he helped me with a term paper I was stressing over. He and his mother were angels sent from the heavens above.

His mother, Ms. Katrina, was the owner of the coffee shop but had to step down to take care of her sick father. Kylan stepped up and took over to help alleviate some of the stress his mother was under. Ms. Katrina still made it her duty to come in every morning and bake her famous blueberry muffins, and giant peanut butter cookies.

Everyone at Milk & Honey viewed her as our mother and loved her dearly. The culture here was like none other. If I could, I'd work here forever, but Kylan made it clear that once I graduated, I needed to find a job in my field.

"Yeah, I promised Jalissa that we would go out tonight," he said with a smile.

"Aww," I gushed.

He'd been with Jalissa for almost a year and they

were the cutest couple, ever. She still came by every morning and he made her a cup of tea. I adored Jalissa. She was the sweetest woman and she treated Kylan well. Ever since they got together, he had an extra pep in his step and spent less time working. I was happy for him.

"Y'all are so cute. I'm a little jealous."

Kylan laughed. "Maybe you'll meet someone tonight."

"Yeah, right! I'm here to host and create romantic vibes. That's *it*!"

"Okay, Mo," he said while shaking his head. "I'm excited to hear how the event goes, though."

A year ago, we had a team meeting and brainstormed events to have throughout the year. Zara and I suggested a speed dating event. I pushed for Valentine's Day because it would give single people something to do, and I'd always wanted to go speed dating. Kylan was on board and asked me to come up with a budget and a proposal. I worked my butt off to create an event that wouldn't hurt our pockets and attract more business.

To say the event was successful would be an understatement. This cute, quaint coffee shop was packed. Since it was our first time having an event since Kylan took over as Manager, we all had to work. It was a busy night, but it increased our traffic and people were eager for the next one. This year we created an online sign-up and stressed that we had limited seating.

While Ms. Katrina and Kylan were pleased with the outcome, they wanted a more intimate event to prevent the staff from experiencing burn out. This year, we would only have thirty attendees, which was a third of the people that came last year. I figured an event this small could be managed on my own, I still preferred Ky here just in case it got hectic.

"I know you're gonna say you can handle tonight, but I asked Jayson to come in and work the speed dating event with you. Before you start whining, I trust you and this event is your baby. However, I can't leave you here to host *and* serve."

Just the sound of Jayson's name made my cheeks warm. Lowering my head, I bit my bottom lip to keep from smiling. Jayson was the newest member of the team, and I had the biggest crush on him. I was sure Kylan knew because when I looked up at him, he was smiling.

"Zara or Nathan couldn't work tonight?" I asked breathlessly.

Kylan shook his head. "Nope. You and Zara wouldn't do anything but laugh and gossip all night. Jayson will stay focused and he makes the best lattes, after me, of course."

"Whatever." I waved him off.

"Don't forget to count the drawer before you leave, and whatever baked goods we don't sell–"

"Put them in the fridge so you can drop them off at

the shelter first thing in the morning. I know, Ky. This isn't my first time closing."

"Tonight, is different though."

"Kylan," I drawled.

"Mocha," he said, mimicking a squeaky voice. I rolled my eyes while folding my arms over my chest. Kylan's eyebrows furrowed as he continued to stare at me. "I can stay until Jayson gets here. What else needs to be done?"

The coffee shop was filled with red and pink balloons, the baked goods Ms. Katrina made were on display, and the menus for tonight were stacked on the counter. Kylan helped me decorate the shop, the only thing left to do was to arrange the tables and mop the floors. That wouldn't take much time and Jayson was scheduled to arrive in less than an hour.

I grabbed his shoulder and smiled. "It'll be fine."

"I'm putting all my trust in you, Mo," he replied with a smirk.

"And I don't take that lightly." I forged a smile even though his admission made my stomach drop.

I was a ball of nerves as I thought about tonight. Knowing I was working with Jayson only made me even more eager for tonight. It was pretty much crush at first sight when I met Jayson. We rarely worked together, though. Jayson was a part-time barista who only worked weekends and holidays. I mostly worked during the week between classes. When I first met Jayson, Kylan was training him. His first test was to make me the perfect mocha latte under Kylan's supervision.

Jayson didn't seem visibly nervous or bothered that Ky and I were watching him as he made my drink. Later, I learned that was just his personality. Always cool, calm, and collected. But he had a funny side too. I'd only seen that side of him a few times. Mostly when we had team outings. Last month, for our holiday party, we went to Top Golf.

The crush I had on him grew after he took it upon himself to be my golf instructor. Everyone was doing well that night, except me. I had more misses than hits. While everyone teased me, Jayson took his role seriously, positioning himself behind me and placing his large hands on top of mine. I could hardly remember any of the advice he gave me. My heart raced as I relished in being in his arms.

"I'll text you to see how everything is going," Ky said as he made his way to the door.

While shaking my head, I replied, "No, don't. Enjoy your night with Jalissa. I've got everything handled."

After Kylan left, I started mopping the floor, so it would be dry by the time the event started. I took a break from mopping and sat down for a moment and looked around the room. A smile covered my lips as I relished in the romantic vibes Kylan and I created for tonight.

Thinking about tonight caused butterflies in the pit

of my stomach. I reached into my apron and grabbed my phone. Zara could've warned me about her not working tonight since she practically stalked the schedule and knew when everyone worked. I suspected it was because she tried to keep up with Nathan's schedule.

Mocha: You could've given me a heads up that you weren't working tonight. :(

Zara: Girl! You know Carlos made plans for us! Who are you working with tonight? Ky isn't staying???

I sighed as I typed my reply.

Mocha: …Jayson

Zara: #JAYBAE?!

While laughing, I nodded as if she could see me.

Mocha: *sigh* Yessss!

Zara: Maybe you'll stop being scary and finally tell him you're madly in love, yeah?

Mocha: Not happening.

There was no way I was putting myself out there like that. Besides, I had no time for a relationship. Finishing school and figuring out the next step was all I had time for.

Zara: You're so stubborn! I have to get ready for my date. You better have some tea for me tomorrow...or else.

I smiled as I read Zara's last message. Instead of crushing her dreams of me having something juicy to share with her, I simply sent a side smirk emoji and put my phone away. With only an hour left before the event started, I started wiping down the tables, smiling as I waited for Jayson to arrive.

☕

As I wiped down the last table, the door chimed and in came Jayson. He looked at me then smiled before removing his coat. My heart was pounding against my chest. It was already bad enough that I had to work with him on Valentine's Day, and he comes here looking as good as ever. He ran his hands over his fresh fade and sighed.

"'Sup, Mo," he crooned as he made his way through the shop.

"Hey," I whispered then shook my head.

He put away his coat in the breakroom then returned. For a moment, he stood at the counter and watched me as I mopped around the makeshift stage Kylan had built.

"What do you need me to do?" he asked.

Without looking at him, I replied, "Move the tables around. I was going to do it but decided to wait until I had more manpower."

He laughed. "Let's wait for the floor to completely dry, then I'll arrange the tables to your liking, cool?"

"Cool." My throat was dry, and I was trying my hardest not to stare into his dreamy espresso colored eyes. Jayson disappeared in the back for a few minutes then returned with his apron and hat on.

"You excited for tonight?" he asked as he started rearranging the tables.

I watched him as he moved the round wooden tables and two chairs on opposite sides. Jayson never wore the apron the way it was supposed to be worn, he folded it in half and tied it around his waist. The same went for the hat, all the men wore. Jayson just had to be different and wear his backward. My eyes continued to admire him from his muscular arms, freshly trimmed goatee, to his seductive slanted eyes.

"More so nervous than excited," I said when I realized he was staring at me.

Jayson leaned on the table across from me with his arms folded over his chest. "No need to be nervous, Mo. Whatever I can do to keep you relaxed, let me know."

"Thanks."

He smirked then nodded. "You ever been speed dating before?" He moved onto the next table while I remained in the same spot utterly enamored by him.

"No, but I've always wanted to! It looks like a lot of fun. What about you?"

Jayson shook his head. "Nah. Speed dating isn't my thing."

"How do you know if you've never done it before?"

"Two minutes isn't enough time for me to get to know someone." He stopped and looked at me. "I've known you for a minute now, and there are still things I want to learn."

I laughed nervously. It was hard to tell whether he

was flirting or being friendly. "I'm an open book," I told him as I pushed off the table.

He grabbed my wrist, pulling me to him. Jayson ran his index finger under my chin and my cheeks warmed. Our lips were mere inches apart. My chest rose and fell as my eyes moved from his eyes to his lips. When his lips curved into a smile, I sighed and took a step back.

"I need to grab something from the supply closet."

Dipping my head, I hurried to the supply closet. I had to get away from Jayson. It felt like the walls were closing in on us.

"Mocha," Jayson called out as he entered the closet.

When I turned to answer him, our lips collided in the most beautiful way. Jayson's lips were warm and sent a shock through me as he gripped my waist drawing me closer to him. It was like our lips were made for one another. After a few exploratory pecks, I tilted my head to the side and parted my lips. My heart raced with anticipation of his tongue meeting mine. The first swipe caused me to moan, then after, I settled into our slow rhythmic kiss. My hands gripped his arms and I smiled at the goosebumps on his arms.

Knowing he was having the same inexplicable reaction I had every time I was around him was gratifying. I could barely believe this was happening. For months, I dreamed about him, how he'd taste, how'd it feel to be in his arms, and it was finally happening. I didn't want it to end. Pressing myself deeper into him, we continued getting acquainted with the feel of each other's lips.

Once Jayson got his fix, he pulled back and looked down at me through heavy lids. My lips were numb from him sucking on them. I broke eye contact with him by lowering my head to hide that I was blushing. Jayson laughed when I started fluffing my hair. Admittedly, I was nervous about what would happen next.

"I couldn't fight it anymore," he said lowly.

Using his index finger, he raised my chin to meet his alluring eyes. My heart was racing at the speed of light and butterflies were swarming through my stomach. Swiping my thumb across my bottom lip. This moment felt surreal. Zara was going to lose her shit when I told her that Jayson kissed me. Jayson smiled, then pressed his lips on my forehead. I exhaled and wrapped my arms around his neck.

"How long have you been feeling like this?"

"Since I made you that mocha latte."

We laughed, mine was more of a nervous giggle.

"What about you?"

"The same day." I shook my head feeling silly for thinking he wouldn't be interested in me. All the signs were there, but I chose to ignore them. hearing him profess him liking me made all apprehensions go away. "Now what?" I asked.

He shrugged. "After we close, let me take you out."

I smiled, wide, like a Cheshire cat. "I'd love that."

Leaning down, Jayson kissed me again, with the same intensity as the first time, leaving me breathless when he pulled back.

"Mo," he said, and I raised my eyebrows, waiting for him to say something. When he didn't answer, my eyebrows drew together.

"Jayson, what's wrong?" I asked.

"Mo!"

My eyes sprung open and I clutched my chest. Looking around, I realized I wasn't in the supply closet. I was in Kylan's office on his futon. Wiping my eyes, I continued to lay there pissed that it was all a damn dream.

Running my thumb across my bottom lip, I still felt the kiss I shared with Jayson. I sighed before sitting up, then pushing my hair from my face. Jayson's footsteps grew louder, and I finally mustered the courage to answer him.

"I'm in the back," I yelled.

I took a series of breaths to calm my racing heart. Before Jayson came back here, I needed to get myself together. We had to work together for the next two hours. Maybe this was a sign that I needed to swallow my pride and shoot my shot.

Jayson stood in the doorway with his coat over his arm. I fluffed my hair and continued to stare ahead as the dream replayed in my mind.

"You good?" He asked with a smile.

Jumping to my feet, I stretched my limbs before brushing past him.

"Yeah. Let's finish setting up." I tossed over my shoulder, avoiding eye contact with him.

2

JAYSON

"Mo!" I yelled from the front of the shop.

The café was completely different from when I was here last week. Balloons filled the room and as I ventured further, I noticed a fresh batch of Ms. Katrina's muffins and cookies were in the display case. I placed the roses I'd gotten for Mo onto the counter and removed my coat. When Kylan hit me up about working tonight, I wasn't exactly thrilled. It was Friday night and while I didn't have plans, I didn't want to spend it watching people flirt and what not.

But then, he mentioned I'd be working with *Mocha*.

I smiled instantly at the sound of her name. Kylan knew I was feeling her. He'd purposely called me instead of Nathan because he knew I'd been avoiding her. Hell, everyone knew except for her. She basically friend-zoned me when I started working here and I hadn't figured out how to recover from that.

After admiring the work she and Kylan had done to get this place ready for tonight, I headed to the back to find *her*.

"I'm in the back," she yelled as I strode the halls in search of her.

I peeked into the supply closet and kitchen she wasn't there. Finally, I went to Kylan's office to find Mo laying on the futon with wide eyes. She sat up and fluffed kinky curls that rested on her shoulders. I loved when Mo wore her hair down. She usually kept her hair in braids that fell at the middle of her back.

"You good?" I asked, smiling.

Jumping to her feet, Mocha stretched her limbs before brushing past me.

"Yeah. Let's finish setting up," she tossed over her shoulder.

Instinctively, my eyes trailed down her frame and I bit my bottom lip. Following close behind her, I listened to the tasks we needed to complete before the attendees arrived.

"I need help with rearranging the tables," she said with furrowed eyebrows when she noticed the roses near the register.

"Those are for you." Her eyes lit up as she grabbed the bouquet and brought it to her nose. "Will you be my Valentine?" I asked as I leaned on the table a few feet away from her.

My heart was pounding in my chest, but I couldn't

let her see me sweat. I wanted to wait until the event was over. That plan went out the window after seeing her for the first time in nearly a month. We texted a few times a week, mostly small talk. Our conversations were always about work or her classes since she was still in school. I didn't want to bore her by talking about my nine to five.

She turned to me with the cutest expression on her face. Mocha's deep brown skin flushed, and doe shaped eyes were wide. My chest tightened as I waited for her to accept my cheesy proposal.

"This is sweet, Jay. I'd love to be your Valentine," she said, tucking her hair behind her ear.

I smiled and reached for her arm. "After we get off, I'm taking you out."

"This is like déjà vu or something," she said, holding her forehead.

"Is this déjà vu too?" I asked, leaning down to meet her lips with mine.

Mocha's lips were just as soft as I imagined. Gripping her chin, I dropped a few pecks on her lips before she tilted her head, allowing me to deepen our kiss. My other hand rested on her waist and Mocha wrapped her arms around my neck, dropping the bouquet onto the table behind me. We created our own rhythm taking turns nipping and sucking the other's bottom lip.

"We need to get ready for tonight," she said after abruptly ending our kiss.

For a few moments more, we stared at each other, my heart rate finally slowed.

"What else do we need to do?" I asked, releasing my hold on her and turning to the remaining tables that needed moving.

Mocha was silent for a beat, then replied, "I think that's all."

Once everything was set, attendees arrived, and Mo turned into the ultimate host. I took my position behind the counter, ready to take orders. Just as the event was set to start, Mo looked at me and I winked. She smiled softly before returning her attention back to the woman she was assisting with finding a table.

☕

*M*ocha sat across from me with the most innocent smile on her face. Since we arrived at *Marcelo's,* that's all we'd been doing. Just staring at one another. The event went by fairly quick. When Mo wasn't serving the guests, she was on the mic making jokes, and keeping everyone entertained.

I stayed behind the counter taking orders and making drinks. It wasn't lost on me she would sneak glances my way when she thought I wasn't paying attention. The few times I made eye contact with her, she bit her bottom lip and her cheeks would turn a tinge of red. I couldn't believe I thought the feelings I had for her were one-sided.

During our ride to the restaurant, she confessed to having a crush on me from the moment we met. I admitted how nervous I was under her and Kylan's watchful eye as I made her drink. We laughed about how we wasted months by being too scared to put ourselves out there. But really the timing couldn't be any more perfect. I started working at Milk & Honey after breaking up with my girlfriend of three years.

The breakup wasn't amicable and left me homeless as the apartment we shared was in her name. I picked up a part-time job to support myself along with my full-time job to find a place as soon as possible. Sleeping on my sister's couch wasn't something I wanted to do for more than a month.

My first day at Milk & Honey wasn't the happiest for me. I was beating myself up for being in a situation where I had to become a barista just to have some extra cash. Kylan was taking a risk by hiring me. I hadn't worked in the fast-food industry since I was in high school. Being true to my word, I picked up on everything fast and proved to Kylan and myself that I could do it.

When I met Mocha, I had no desire to date or be in a relationship. The shit I went through with my ex was still heavy on my mind. I guess that was how we settled into an easy friendship.

"You never told me how it ended," Mocha said as the waiter brought our drinks.

Somehow the conversation shifted from when we

realized our attraction for one another to past relationships. It had been six months since Jina and I broke up. Our sudden separation blindsided me. We weren't on the same page and I didn't realize it until it was too late. I thought marriage was in the near future. I had picked the ring out and payments were about to be made.

On our third anniversary, Jina told me she was unhappy and had been for a long time. Apparently, our relationship had become too routine and boring. Knowing that I was coming home to her every day was enough for me. Listening to her day as we cooked dinner together was the highlight of my day. To her, it was unexciting. Jina claimed our relationship lacked passion. The ring in my pocket felt like a boulder, the more she listed her complaints about our relationship.

"On our third anniversary, she said she was no longer happy. Our relationship became boring and routine," I answered honestly.

Mocha's lips turned downward, and eyebrows drew together. "I'm so sorry," she told me as she reached for my hand.

"It's cool. I'm happy that everything happened when it did. I was ready to propose. That night was the sign I needed that she wasn't the one."

"Are you still in love with her?"

"Nah," I told her. "Not anymore."

Mocha nodded and then looked over the menu. Tonight, Marcelo's had a special four-course menu for Valentine's Day. After we placed our orders, Mocha remained silent. For the first time tonight, I became a little insecure about my past. Here I was trying to start something new, but sharing that six months ago, I was ready to propose to someone else.

"I didn't kill the mood, did I?" I asked.

Mocha shook her head. "I was engaged once."

My eyebrows shot up. She'd just turned twenty-one a few months ago. It was shocking to hear that she'd been in the same position I was once in.

"What happened?"

"I was eighteen and fresh out of high school. He was about to leave for school, and he knew the only way I'd go with him is if we were married." She shook her head and scoffed. "Back then, I thought it was the most romantic thing ever. In reality, it was manipulative as hell. But I was young and naïve, so I went. Never did I think it would lead to him becoming this controlling person I didn't know. I was lucky to have left when I did."

I sat back in my seat, a sigh pressing through my lips.

"I've pretty much been single ever since," she admitted, her eyes glossy and filled with vulnerability.

Another gaping silence fell over us. After hearing about Mocha's last relationship, I now understood why we both were so reluctant to put ourselves out there. Out of all the conversations we had in the past, this one was the most eye-opening.

"Wanna hear something funny?" she asked, after a moment.

"Shoot."

"Today, I had a dream we kissed in the supply closet."

I smiled. "What else happened?"

"Actually, you woke me up, so I didn't get to finish it. But tonight, this date is far better than the dream I had. I just hope this," Mocha waved her hand between us, "doesn't end tonight."

Shaking my head, I replied, "Not at all. It took me months to muster up the courage to be real about my feelings for you. This is just the first of many dates."

Her cheeks turned red and I smiled. The way she reacted to me would never get old.

"You work every day. When will you have time to take me on dates?" she asked, with a hint of amusement in her tone.

It was true; I worked six days out of the week, but my evenings and Sundays would belong to her. Adjusting my schedule to include her wouldn't be a problem and should be the least of her worries.

"Don't worry about that. I'll always have time for you."

"Pinch me."

"This isn't a dream, Mo," I said, laughing.

"I just need to make sure!" She fell back in her seat and laughed.

Leaning over the table, I pressed my lips against

hers. Her hand went to my cheek as she held me in place. A quiet whimper came from her when I sucked her bottom lip. Slowly, I pulled back and looked at her. Her mesmerizing orbs pulled at my heart, making me smile.

"This is only the beginning, babe."

CINNAMON GIRL

CYNARA

Why am I doing this?

The question I'd been asking myself the entire drive to Milk & Honey Café. I needed to stop listening to my best friend, Nicole. It was because of her; I was on my way to something I'd regret. I shook my head as I turned off my car. This was my second year being single on Valentine's Day, and while I wasn't feeling lonely or unloved, I was *somewhat* ready to get back out there and start dating.

I spent the past two years focusing on finishing my doctorate and getting settled into my career. During that time, the dating scene had changed. My friends were using dating apps and shared their horror stories.

Because of them, I vowed to stay off dating apps and try to find love the old-fashioned way.

Nicole and I came to Milk and Honey at least three times a week. It was Black-owned, and the service was excellent. Last week, Nicole saw the flyer for speed dating, and of course, my single ass was the first person who came to mind. While she was out with her husband eating a four-course meal, I would have dull conversations with men I knew didn't interest me. It took days for her to convince me to give speed dating a try.

After all, she met Lawrence at a networking event five years ago and had been blissfully in love ever since. She even used their story to persuade me. I still wasn't sure how speed dating and a networking event were synonymous, but whatever. It was this or taking myself out on another solo date. After touching up my lipstick, I headed inside to find a seat. The barista and hostess for the evening, Mo, showed me to my numbered table and took my order.

"I'll be right back with your latte and a muffin," she said before walking away.

I glanced around the room while fidgeting my nails. Looking down, I admired my fresh gel manicure and the silver rings that adorned my dainty fingers. A few moments passed before Mo came back with my drink and a blueberry muffin. Nervously, I ran my hands down my braids and sighed. This coffee shop was cute. I was used to the smell of roasted coffee beans and jazzy music filling the air.

Tonight, the shop was filled with red heart-shaped balloons and confetti covered the table. There was sultry music coming from the in-ceiling speakers that added to the romantic ambiance. There were a few handsome men here, all waiting for the event to start. I took a sip of my cinnamon spiced latte and sighed again.

I wasn't too sure if I was up for having five-minute dates for the next two hours. The women on both sides of me looked eager for the night to begin. Meanwhile, I was trying to calm my nerves and prayed the knot in my stomach would go away.

"These men are *extra* fine tonight," the woman to my left leaned over and said to me.

I nodded, then took a bite out of my muffin. Glancing her way, I looked over her appearance. She was ready for whatever the night brought. Her dress was sexy, heels were high, and her makeup was on *point*.

"Last year was packed. I guess because it was the first time they had the event. The dates were shorter. Like two minutes. Hardly enough time to get to know someone!"

It was called *speed* dating for a reason, but I guess she took this far more seriously than I did.

"Any luck last year?" I asked absentmindedly. I was wondering if this was for real connections and serious dating or just a Valentine's Day hookup thing.

"Yeah, actually," she breathed. "We dated for a few months, but once summer rolled around, things kind of fell off." She shrugged then sipped what looked like tea.

"I hope tonight is different, though. I'm not looking for anything serious this time around. Just trying to end the night with someone, you know?"

Offering her a weak smile, I brought my mug to my lips so I wouldn't have to answer her. I wasn't looking for the love of my life or a hookup. Hell, I was still trying to figure out why I was here. Just as she was about to continue, Mo walked onto the stage and grabbed the mic.

"Alright, guys. Each date is five minutes, I will let you all know when it's time to switch. To keep things interesting, we have given all the men cards with questions on them. If you ever get shy or are having trouble starting a conversation, take a quick look at the card. I promise they will keep the convo going. Good luck!" she threw pink confetti in the air and giggled before leaving the stage.

The music resumed and my first date sauntered over to me. He was... *okay*.

Looked to be about five-foot-ten, slim frame, and... a receding hairline. The gray plaid suit he wore was a little too big, and there were wrinkles in his pants.

Oh, God!

I adjusted my posture as he neared my table.

Gosh, how old was this man? Nicole said this event was for Millennials. He was giving me *Generation X-er*. Date number one remained silent as he pulled out his chair and took a seat. A few seconds ticked by before he made eye contact with me. Immediately, he looked at the card, and I sighed.

"Hi, I'm Cyn," I said, holding out my hand.

"Ron," he replied before sliding his clammy hand onto mine.

I wiped my hand on my dress then took another sip of my drink.

I'm going to kill Nicole.

"I-If you could go to any country and live for a year where would you go and why?"

He couldn't be serious. Ron's gaze was still on the red card in his hand. My eyes moved from his hands to his receding hairline. There were a few grays in his hair, further confirming my suspicions that he was at least fifty.

A few moments passed before I conceded and answered his question.

"The Maldives. I'm saving to go next summer. What about you?"

"Jamaica."

"I've been a few times, and I loved it."

He nodded and continued to look at the card. My eyebrows furrowed as I glared at Ron. If this was how speed dating went, I wouldn't be staying after the intermission. I had better things to do with my time. Leaning back into my seat, I looked around the room and felt slightly envious at the people who were engaged in meaningful conversation. Homegirl beside me was more entertaining than the man in front of me. So far, she'd gotten every detail about her date except his social security number.

Her date's non-verbal cues showed how attracted he was to her. Every time she spoke, his eyes moved from her eyes to her lips. He laughed at her corny jokes and even grabbed her hand a few times. We were only two minutes into our date and she'd already found someone to end the night with!

My attention returned to Ron, he was slouched over, staring at the card.

"What's the next question?" I asked exasperatedly.

Clearing his throat, he asked, "How many sexual partners have you had?"

A guttural laugh fell from my lips before I could stop myself. "You can't even make eye contact with me, but you want to know my sexual history? Next question."

I noticed his sienna colored skin flushed at my dismissal. He had some nerve asking about my past. If I hadn't started the introduction, he wasn't even going to tell me his name. He chewed on his bottom lip as he continued to look at the card.

"Let me see that," I said, snatching the card from him.

After doing a quick scan, I realized that wasn't even a question. I threw the card back toward Ron and stormed to the bathroom. I paced back and forth in the two-stall bathroom as I tried to calm my racing heart. Once I calmed down, I relieved my bladder, then washed my hands. Hopefully, when I returned, there would be someone worth chatting with sitting at my table.

Lord knows I didn't have the patience to deal with another Ron. I wet a paper towel and patted my face. That jerk really pissed me off. If men were this forward, maybe I should continue to live the "single life." I lingered in the bathroom a few moments longer until I heard Mo tell the men to switch tables. A long, slow exhale pressed through my lips as I adjusted my dress and fixed my hair. With my head held high, I strutted back to my table.

Date number two looked more promising. He wore a navy blazer that stretched across his broad shoulders. His posture was perfect as he sat with his back facing me. I smiled at the sight of his shiny bald head. At least he wasn't in denial like Ron and cut it off before it was too late.

With a smile, I grabbed his shoulder and said, "Sorry to keep you waiting."

My stomach jumped when he turned to face me.

"Cynara Martin," Lennox Jackson said as he stood to hug me.

"How have you been?" I asked, accepting his embrace.

He took a step back, his arm still on my waist, and smiled. "Good, but not as good as you."

"Still a charmer." I took my seat across from him and continued smiling.

Lennox and I dated my senior year of college. We both knew our lives would lead to different paths after graduation, instead of trying to force it, we went our separate ways. He was finishing up his master's degree, and I was preparing for grad school, the location was undetermined at that time.

We were both career-focused and goal-oriented back then, and nothing, not even love, could get in the way. Lennox was a great guy and an even better lover. The timing just wasn't right. Our breakup was mutual and for a while, we kept in touch. As time passed, our phone calls became few and far between, and eventually ceased. I still checked his Instagram every once and a while, though.

"It's been what? Six years?" he asked, still in awe. His mahogany eyes showed a glint of lust. Leaning forward, his smile widened, making my stomach knot and pussy throb.

"Yes, it has. I thought you were in San Francisco. That's why we fell off, you know?"

He chuckled. His deep timbre still affects me the same way it did six years ago. My eyes raked over him. I always loved his rich, hickory colored skin. It was damn near perfect, not a blemish or bump in sight. Undoubtedly, he'd gotten finer over the years. I thought he was good looking before. Lennox from college didn't have shit on grown man Lennox.

"I'm still out there." He caressed his beard, his eyes boring into mine. "I come home every now and then."

"You could never sit still," I quipped, making him laugh.

He shook his head. "Nah. Now I'm wondering if leaving was a mistake."

His mahogany orbs darkened, and I damn near melted in my seat. "How long are you in town?"

"A couple more weeks. I have a few meetings out here with our partners. I would've never pegged you to be the type to do this." He waved his hand, a grin covering his lips.

I shrugged. "Trying something different. What about you?"

"You've always been adventurous," he teased. "A few days ago, I stopped by to grab some breakfast and saw the flyer. I figured this would be more interesting than going to my hotel's bar." His gaze did a quick sweep over me. "Seems like I made the right decision." Lennox swiped his tongue across his bottom lip, and I sucked in a breath. My body tingled as memories of the way he used to have my body humming came to mind.

I waited until I "fell in love" before having sex. I was twenty when I lost my virginity. The experience was something I wish I could forget. After I broke up with my first love, I waited until I found someone I could be more willing to let me explore my sexuality. Lennox was my second sexual encounter.

Our sexual chemistry was explosive and other-worldly. I felt like I was behind sexually and wanted to make up for the lost time. Lennox was patient and taught me a lot. To this day, he's still one of my best partners. Crossing my legs, I leaned forward and licked my lips.

"I'm even more adventurous now," I whispered.

His hand went under the table as he adjusted in his seat. "I'm sure."

My bottom lip hurt from biting down so hard. Lennox's sex appeal was unmatched. He didn't have to do much to turn me on, just like back then.

"Are you going to ask me some questions?" I asked, nodding toward the red card on the table.

Lennox shook his head. "The questions I have aren't listed on that card."

I giggled and covered my mouth. My braids fell over my shoulder when I tilted my head to the side. "Well, what do you want to ask me?"

"What have you been up to? How many degrees do you have now?"

A smile played at the corners of my mouth as I thought about the conversations we had advanced degrees. Right now, I was getting my doctorate in public health. If it weren't for my job paying a little over fifty percent, I'd be shit out of luck.

"Two. I'm working on the third one now."

"I knew you'd go for the doctorate."

Waving my hand, I said, "Yes, you were right. Back then, it seemed like too much, but once I got my masters, I was like, why not?" I shrugged.

Leaning back in his seat, Lennox spread his legs and

with the sexiest smirk on his lips. Whatever question he asked next, my answer would undoubtedly be yes.

"Tell me, Cynara. What's a man got to do to get back in touch with you?"

Mo came over with a smile interrupting my dirty thoughts. "Would you like another latte?"

"Still hooked on them cinnamon-spiced lattes, huh?" Lennox mused, a small smile resting on his lips.

Looking at Mo, I replied, "Yes, please."

"And you, sir?" she asked Lennox.

"I'm fine, sweetheart."

She nodded before walking away. Lennox and I stared at each other for a few moments before I finally looked away. I looked around the cafe, wondering how much time I had left with him. I was sure that after this date, every other one would be a waste of time.

"You didn't answer my question," he said after a beat.

"My number is still the same," I shot back with a grin.

"I have a new phone and a new number." He pulled his phone from his pocket and slid it across the table. "While I'm here, we should go out for dinner."

After saving my number, I slid the phone back to him. "Yeah, maybe."

I saw Mo coming our way with my drink; she checked the time on her watch and looked around the room. It was then that I realized our time was now winding down.

"It was good seeing you," I said.

"The feeling is mutual. Don't worry, we'll see each other again soon." He reached across the table for my hand. Slowly, he brought my hand to his soft, full lips, causing a chill to jolt down my spine and goosebumps to cover my warm skin.

We continued to stare as Mo placed my cup on the table and made her way to the mic. A small sigh pressed through my lips as she made the announcement to switch. My eyes stayed on Lennox as he sauntered to the next table. My new date sat down, a smile covering his lips. With a sigh, I gave him and every date after that, my full attention.

2

LENNOX

I let Cynara slip away from me once, and I wasn't about to let it happen again. At first, I was on the fence about going speed dating. One, I wasn't looking for a relationship. Two, I didn't plan on being in town long enough to explore anything past a five-minute date.

But then I saw *her*.

Running into her tonight was pure happenstance and I refused to let the few minutes we shared be the only time I got to spend with her.

My last date of the evening was having a hard time catching the hint that not only was she not going home with me, but we also weren't exchanging numbers either. While she continued to flirt, I searched the room for Cynara.

Cynara Martin was the one woman who kept me on my shit and made me want to have it all together sooner than later. She was the kind of woman who made you want to be the best version of yourself. I recognized that six years ago and since then; I hadn't met a woman like her. Cynara had always been goal-oriented and super focused on having a successful career.

I admired her work ethic and her drive. She didn't play with her future and what she wanted to do. Unfortunately, our relationship goals didn't align and because of that, we had to part ways. Promising to keep in touch was easier said than done. Between the time differences and workloads, falling off was inevitable. There wasn't a day I didn't think about her, though. Trying to stay up to date via her social media was cool, but I was interested in what her life was like offline.

I half-expected her to be married with a kid by now. A woman like Cynara was one that could get snatched up quickly. She knew her worth and wasn't afraid to let you know it. My friends thought she was too head-strong, but I loved that shit. I didn't want a meek part-ner, and Cynara was everything I wanted and then some. She made even the coldest man want to try love. Cyn was like a cup of hot cider on a cold winter night. She soothed and warmed my soul. Having her as my lady was a privilege I didn't appreciate until after I lost her.

This wasn't an opportunity I'd take for granted. Nah, I would enjoy as much of her as I could. And when I returned to San Francisco, I would hold up my end of the deal by calling and texting, as necessary.

"So, what do you say?" Lisa, I *think* that was her

name, said to me with her bottom lip tucked between her teeth and head tilted to the side. I stopped looking around the room and finally gave her eye contact. Her smile was flirty as she ran her fingers down the lapel of my blazer. I offered her a half-smile before gently shooting her down.

"Not tonight, love," I said.

"Well, maybe another time. Hit me up next time you're in town." She took my phone from the pocket of my blazer and saved her number. I nodded, already knowing that I'd never make use of her number. Not having a passcode on my phone was a mistake, one I'd correct once I got back to my hotel tonight.

When Lisa finally released my arm, I walked outside the quaint coffee shop for Cynara. I smiled as I watched her strut toward her car. The confidence she exuded was palpable.

"Cyn," I yelled out as I jogged down the sidewalk to her. She turned around, smiling then leaned on the side of her car. "Come to my spot… for a nightcap."

Her smile widened as she weighed her options. I continued to take her in. From her smooth cinnamon colored skin to those cute freckles that were sprinkled across her nose and cheeks still did something to me. And her lips, man. She had the sexiest natural pout. My eyes lowered to her hips, she always had a little curve on her frame.

"Okay," she said, "*one* drink."

I smiled. "Yeah, one drink."

ynara looked around my room with an unreadable expression. I took off my blazer and shoes, making myself comfortable before I went to the minibar to see what we were working with. Going to the hotel bar was out of the question. It was a little party happening down there and I needed Cynara's undivided attention. She definitely had mine. I watched her take a seat on the couch, crossing one leg over the other.

"You still drink whiskey?" I asked as I poured myself a glass. She nodded then walked over to me. After pouring her a glass, I handed it to her. She held the glass at her lips for a second before taking a sip. Cynara's sex appeal was second to none. Part of me felt weakened from the visceral reaction I had with her.

"I can't believe you were speed dating," she said with a chuckle.

"I can say the same for you. I just knew you'd be off the market by now."

She shook her head. "A woman like me isn't in high demand these days."

"Shit," I drawled. "I beg to differ."

"You didn't want me when you had me," she teased.

After taking a gulp of my drink, I replied, "That's not true and you know it."

While running her finger along the rim of her drink,

she said, "I know, I know the 'timing' wasn't right. It still isn't right."

"How you figure?"

"I'm here and you're across the country. Plus, we've changed. Who's saying it would work out this time?"

"Me."

Cynara rolled her eyes and went back to her spot on the sofa. "You don't have to sell me dreams to have sex."

"I'm not selling dreams."

"Okay," she said in a sing-song tone. "What happened with Farrah?"

My eyebrows shot up and lip twisted. It seems like I wasn't the only one keeping tabs via social media. "She said I work too much. What about you and what's his name?"

She giggled because she knew how much I hated her ex, Kendal. It started when I was a teacher's assistant for their senior seminar class. Kendal was a pain in my ass, always asking for extensions on assignments and extra credit. It disappointed me to learn they started dating a year after I moved away. Adding further insult to injury, they lasted for nearly five years.

"You remember how Kendal was in school? Well, he was the same after graduation. He had no real goals or ambitions. That didn't work for me. I wasted so much time trying to change him. I thought if he saw how hard I was grinding, he'd do the same, but it didn't work out that way. Oh well, his loss," she said matter-of-factly.

"I can't say that I'm surprised that he hasn't changed." I paused, contemplating whether I wanted to continue this conversation. Falling down the dark hole of past relationships wasn't something I wanted to get into tonight. Switching gears, I asked, "Did you enjoy speed dating? Any prospects?"

With a chuckle, she replied, "If there were any prospects, I wouldn't be here." She sighed. "For the most part, I enjoyed myself. After you, the dates got better."

Cyn explained how creepy her first date acted. She was about to call it a night when she returned from the bathroom, but after seeing me she stayed to the end. She changed her mind once we settled into our conversation. I was glad I was the reason she stayed and that she agreed to leave with me.

"What about you?" she asked, curiosity lingering in her eyes.

"I made one connection." Cyn quirked her eyebrows and leaned forward. There was no way she didn't know I was talking about her. Even after our date, I kept an eye on her. I watched as she conversed with her dates, laughed at their jokes, and the subtle way she flirted with them. I was too enraptured with her to pay my dates any attention. "Well, more like reconnection, but I feel like she's playing hard to get."

She laughed while rolling her eyes. "Come on, Lennox. Let's just accept this for what it is."

And what's that?"

Cyn and this tough girl act was funny. Deep down, she was a lover. It was apparent that Kendal had hurt her in ways I wasn't privy to yet. If she gave me a chance, I would put the pieces of her heart back together and show her the love she deserved.

"One last night."

Before I could respond, Cynara straddled my lap. Her eyes were low and enticing. My hands went to her waist as I held her in place. A smirk covered her lips and I gripped her waist tighter. I had a few hours to convince her this was more than just a fling. Maybe I was thinking too deep into it, but us bumping into each other tonight was meant to be more than a night of pleasure. She didn't give me a chance to protest before her lips were on mine. Remnants of the whiskey lingered on her lips mixed with her naturally sweet taste.

I wrapped her braids around my hand, tilting her head back. While I dropped kisses down her neck, she ground against me. Using my free hand, I gripped her thigh, pushing her dress over her hips.

"Remember when I used to visit you during office hours?" she asked between panting.

While smiling against her collarbone, I nodded. Cynara let me have her anytime, anyplace. She was always willing to try new things, whether it be new positions, where we had sex, or what we used during sex. As I continued to kiss and suck her neck and chest, I reached behind her for my glass.

I took out a cube of ice and placed it in her mouth to

suck. She slid the straps of her dress off her shoulder, exposing her breasts. After, I ran the cube from her collarbone to her breasts. Once her nipple hardened, I captured it with my mouth, running slow circles around it with my tongue. Her nails dug into my shoulder as I rubbed the other nipped with the cube of ice. Once the cube melted, I moved to the other breast taking my time sucking, nibbling, and licking while she rocked against me.

"Tell me what you want, Cynara," I said in her ear. Her body quivered and grip on my shoulder tightened. Using the pads of my fingertips, I ran my hand up her thigh to the seat of her panties. I slid them to the side and pressed my thumb on her clit. A grin covered my lips when her back arched and stomach pressed against mine. "That's it, huh?"

She nodded and moaned quietly. I used my other hand and gripped her braids tighter. Cynara gazed at me through heavy lids, her chest rose and fell, and her mouth formed an "o" when I slid two fingers into her. My thumb stayed on her clit, rubbing circles.

"You didn't tell me what you want, love," I said.

"This is what I want." She reached between us and gripped my dick.

I grinned then took her bottom lip into my mouth. Her hand moved up and down over my slacks then she unzipped them. After releasing her hair and removing my hand from her lap, I sat back and watched Cynara work. She moved from my lap and onto her knees. My dick was in her direct line of sight. A mischievous smirk rested on her lips as she continued to stroke me. I closed my eyes at the feeling of her tongue on my head.

She continued to stroke me as her warm mouth covered me, her tongue moving continuously around my head. My stomach tightened and I pressed my eyes tighter. Cynara knew what she was doing, and she knew I was slowly becoming undone. I couldn't go out like that, though. Slowly, I rocked my hips and met the back of her throat. She moaned and I swear I almost lost it.

With a satisfied expression on her face, she stood and asked for a condom. I reached in my pocket and retrieved one before removing my pants. Cynara undressed then positioned herself over me. She took the condom from me and sheathed me. With her eyes glued to mine, she slid down slowly. Both of us exhaled in pleasure before kissing.

Everything about tonight felt unreal. First bumping into her at Milk & Honey, then her coming back to my room, and now this. I expected to end tonight alone while watching highlights on Sports Center. Instead, I had Cynara bouncing up and down on my dick. Her nails digging into my flesh, beads of sweat dripping down her spine as she continued to ride me into oblivion.

I grabbed her neck and brought her lips down to mine. Her hips moved faster and moans grew louder as our tongues lashed against one another. Wrapping my arm around her waist, I flipped us over and hooked her legs over my shoulders. I latched onto her clit, sucking and slurping until I felt her juices cover my mouth and beard. She tasted as good as I remembered. Steadily Cyn rocked her hips onto my mouth, I continued to devour her while her orgasm took over. I peered up at her and smiled at the satiated expression on her face.

Cynara grabbed my face and kissed me, sucking the remnants of her from my mouth. After taking a deep plunge into her wetness, I delivered her hard, steady strokes. Strokes that had her legs shaking and words slurring.

"Right… there," Cyn whimpered.

I smiled in the crook of her neck before nipping it.

Her waist rocked against me and breaths quickened. I knew what was coming next. Using my thumb, I drew slow circles on her clit. The grip she had on my shoulders tightened, and her warmth surrounded me as a sharp cry fell from her lips.

My peak came shortly after hers, then we kissed like it would be the last kiss we ever shared. Her lips were red and swollen, only adding to her sex appeal. We laid on the couch in silence; all that was heard was our breathing. My mind racing about what would happen next. I was too tired to tackle that topic tonight, though.

Cynara ran her fingers down my chest to my stomach.

"Round two?" she asked sweetly.

"Whatever you want," I replied as she led me to the bed.

3

CYNARA

The sheets smelled like *him.*

A chill shot through me as memories of last night filled my mind. My night with Lennox was everything I needed and more. I grabbed the robe he left on the chair for me and searched the suite for him. After realizing he was gone, I hurried into the bathroom and used the toothbrush he left for me. Part of me was glad he wasn't here. I couldn't take the post-sex talk. No matter how great last night was, I had to remember that was it.

Lennox and I already tried, and it didn't work out. Rekindling what we had didn't seem realistic, mainly since he lived thousands of miles away.

As quickly as I could, I got dressed and grabbed my phone and purse. Before leaving, I wrote a note thanking Lennox for last night. This wasn't my style at all. I barely knew what to say and laughed at myself when I read back the note I'd written to him. My phone rang and I jumped, thinking it was him. I shook my head before answering Nicole's call.

"I'm guessing speed dating went well. You didn't text me when you got in."

Smiling, I replied, "It did."

"Spill it!" she shrieked in my ear.

"Long story short, I ran into my college boyfriend. I'm trying to sneak out before he comes back!"

She giggled. "Ooh, Cynara! I didn't know you had it in you."

Rolling my eyes, I said, "I'll call you when I get home, for real this time!"

"Please do! I need all the details."

"Bye, crazy," I said before hanging up. Before leaving, I did one last sweep under the bed to make sure I didn't forget anything. The sound of the door opening made my heart drop.

"Heading out?" he asked, smiling.

"Yes."

I noticed he was holding a tray and a bag. Knowing that he left out to get us breakfast and coffee made me feel even worse for trying to slip out.

"Damn, you weren't going to say bye?"

Pointing toward the desk, I replied, "I wrote a note."

Lennox walked past me to the desk and read the note aloud. "Thanks for last night. Hope to see you again?" His voice fell flat and left brow rose. I shrugged with a half-smile. My entire body grew warm under his scruti-nous glare. "Really, Cyn? You were gonna dip out like I was some booty call?" He tossed the pad onto the table and sat the tray of drinks and a white paper bag down.

"I didn't know what else to do."

"Wait for me to come back, maybe?" He took a seat on the couch and shook his head. "I went to Milk & Honey and got you a latte and a muffin."

"Lennox, last night was great, but we have to be realistic."

"Just admit you're scared," he said.

"Scared?"

His mahogany orbs darkened, and eyebrows furrowed. "C'mon, Cyn. I don't know what happened between you and Kendal, but it has you guarded. That isn't the woman I knew six years ago."

"I told you I've changed," I said, folding my arms over my chest.

Lennox stood and walked over to me. "Nah, you're still the same. You're just putting up a front. You still like to be held in your sleep, you're still witty, and you still want me," he said, backing me into the door.

He was right.

I did still want him, but there was that tiny part of me that remembered how I felt when he left. I never told Lennox that I wanted him to stay. It wasn't fair to him. Trying to keep in touch wasn't easy. Every day I felt him slipping from me. His new life in San Francisco became a priority. I decided, letting him go was easier than trying to find my place in his new life.

"How is this supposed to work?" I asked with furrowed eyebrows. "You'll whisk me off my feet while you're here, then when you leave, it'll be like the last time."

Lennox gripped my chin and pressed his lips against mine. "I'm not the guy you were with six years ago. I know how to make time for what's important now. You think I'd fuck up twice?" He laughed. "Nah. I learned my lesson the first time."

He kissed me again before going to eat his muffin. I remained still by the door mulling over his words.

"C' mere, Cyn," he said in between bites. Once I was in front of him, he pulled me onto his lap. "We don't have to figure everything out today. Enjoy your latte, then we'll go to your place so you can shower. After that, I'm taking you out on a real date."

All I could do was smile and drink my latte.

*L*ennox Jackson was one *hell* of a man. Posted on the trunk of his car in a hoodie and jeans, I gripped my bag tighter before running to him. The last three months were excruciating. We talked and texted all day, every day, but it wasn't the same as being in his arms. Smelling his musky cologne, feeling the hairs of his beard tickle my cheek as we hugged, or kissing him. God, his kisses, I craved them while we were apart.

He looked up from his phone and smiled instantly when he saw me. When I was in his reach, he picked me up, then spun me around. My cheeks hurt from smiling so hard. I'd been counting down the days until I could see him again.

What better way to celebrate my birthday than with him?

The months we spent apart gave us a chance to get to know each other again. Lennox had grown so much since I was in college. Don't get me wrong, he was a good man back then, but now, he was literally perfect, for me. Nights when I would be stressed over my dissertation, he'd listen to me whine, then talk me through it. That was the support I needed and missed.

Giving us a second chance was the best decision I made. After going speed dating, of course. Nicole didn't let a day go by without reminding me she got Lennox and me back together. The glow I had these days was unmistakable. I hadn't felt this secure with a man in a long time. Which was crazy to me because he wasn't within reach.

I couldn't wait to spend the next week with him. Once I returned home, I would wrap up my dissertation and prepare for graduation. This time with him was desperately needed.

"I missed you, baby," he said in my ear. Goosebumps dotted my skin as he dropped warm kisses along my jawline.

"I missed you more."

"Show me how much you missed me."

With a smile, I said, "Oh, I plan to."

COFFEE ON THE ROOF

1

ZARA

"I can't ever depend on you," I yelled as tears fell from my eyes. Looking over my shoulder, I made sure no one was coming before continuing, "I'm tired of you taking advantage of me. Sick of it! Carlos, I let you use my car under one condition, that you'd pick me up on time. You're an hour late!" My voice echoed into the night.

There was no use in me leaving a long message. Carlos wasn't going to listen to it and he for damn sure wasn't calling me back tonight.

Why did I continue to torment myself like this?

Carlos had proven many times he wasn't the one for me, yet I sat here foolishly waiting for him to do a complete one-eighty.

I was the literal definition of insanity right now.

Nothing about this situation was healthy. The longer

I stayed with him, the more scorned I became. The arguments were redundant, and at this point, I'd rather be alone than arguing about the same person over and over.

This morning we had an argument about the mother of his children. She called him whenever she wanted, and I told him it was disrespectful to me and our relationship. It was no secret that she was still in love with him. You would think after three years, she would've moved on by now, but no, she was still holding onto the past. No matter how much I complained about her calls, Carlos did nothing to stop her. And he didn't want me to approach her, saying it could prevent him from seeing his children.

This entire situation was exhausting, and I'd undoubtedly reached my breaking point. I would never make him choose between his children or me. That seemed selfish and after growing up with parents who hated each other, I had a soft spot for his children, and I empathize with their situation.

With my arms wrapped around me, I hung my head low. I held myself tighter as I heaved a sigh and trembled as a cool breeze blew past me. While running upstairs to the rooftop of my job, I forgot to grab my jacket. I hadn't realized I was standing in the cold until goosebumps dotted my skin, and I shivered. The long-sleeved shirt I wore did nothing to keep me warm.

I needed to head back inside and finish my closing duties before calling a ride to take me home, but I couldn't let my coworker, Nathan, see me like this. If I were closing with Mocha, I would've been crying on her shoulder as I explained what happened. But tonight, out of all nights, Kylan scheduled me with Nathan, also known as "my gentle giant."

It was a nickname me and Mo had secretly given him. He was a big dude, but the kindest soul I'd ever met. Since my first day at Milk & Honey, he'd been the best coworker and I considered him a friend, too. We could talk about almost anything. My relationship with Carlos was a topic we both skirted around. Nathan and Kylan warned me about Carlos early on. A lot of my other friends and family, did too, but I refused to listen to them, accusing them of being overprotective and judgmental.

Truthfully, Carlos had shown me his true colors early in our relationship. I was so blinded by love, or maybe I was just plain stupid, but I kept giving him chance after chance. But after the argument we had this morning and him ignoring me all day, we were done. A few days from now, he'd come around and beg for my forgiveness. That was our cycle. We argued, he would apologize, then he showered me with gifts for weeks. I was tired of arguing; him being sorry, and the gifts used to pacify me until the next time he screwed up.

I deserved better, period.

"What are you doing out here?" Nathan's baritone bellowed into the night.

I jumped at the sound of his voice. Quickly, I wiped away my tears then turned to face him. He had a small smile on his lips, but his eyebrows were drawn together. In his hands were my coat, a thermos, and two mugs. After a brief stare-off he walked over to me. I heaved a sigh once he got closer. Part of me was happy he came up here. I could use his calming energy right now.

After handing me my coat, he poured us a cup of coffee. I put on my coat and sniffled as he continued to stare at me. I couldn't bring myself to look at him. If I did, I felt like he'd know Carlos did something. Nathan was weird like that. He had the gift of reading people. The longer he stared at me, the more uncomfortable I became.

"You made another special drink?" I asked him to avoid his question.

Finally, I looked at him and caught his heavy gaze. Nathan nodded his head while smiling at me.

God, his smile was beautiful. The dimple in his left cheek showed itself, and my skin warmed. I reached for the mug closest to me and took a sniff, and the smell of cinnamon filled my nostrils, causing a smile to cover my lips.

"Snickerdoodle latte," he said, his eyes still pinned on me.

"Kylan needs to bring this back."

I took a sip and moaned. Nathan nodded again as he took a sip of his drink. He pressed his elbows on the cemented banister and looked at the sky. Kylan and Jayson always said they were the best baristas in the shop, but Nathan was my favorite by far. Something about the way he made his drinks were different.

On the nights that we closed, we had one last cup of coffee on the roof of Milk & Honey. Usually, it would be well after we completed our closing duties, but tonight, I needed some fresh air... and I needed to call Carlos.

I never told Nathan that I looked forward to our coffee dates. They were the perfect way to end my long days. Between going to school full time, work-study, and working at Milk & Honey, I hardly had a second to breathe. Our dates allowed me to decompress before going home. Most nights, I didn't know what I'd have to deal with once I left here.

"So, are you ready to tell me why you've been crying?"

I sucked in a breath and slowly exhaled. Bringing my mug to my lips, I took another sip of my drink and shook my head.

"No, but I have a feeling we're not leaving until I do."

He chuckled lowly, making my stomach flip and heart race. "I mean, if you want to stand in the cold all night, I don't mind." Nathan stuffed his hands into his coat pocket and changed his stance. Now, his back rested on the banister. "You're always sayin' how much you hate winter, but you've been up here for a good twenty minutes."

"Just needed some fresh air."

"Yeah?" He didn't sound too convinced.

"Yeah. That's all."

"Why were you cryin' then?"

My gaze fell to the ground. The "broken-hearted girl" act was hard when I had Nathan's fine ass staring down at me with furrowed eyebrows and penetrating hazel eyes. Mo and I concluded he was the finest one here, Jayson was in second place. We didn't even consider Kylan he was like our annoying big brother. Nathan's six-foot-five frame excited a petite woman like me.

Trying to keep my thoughts, PG was hard, especially when I was always on the outs with Carlos. The attraction I had for Nathan was beyond the physical. He was a great listener and full of jokes. His honey colored skin, hazel eyes, and thick beard were just the icing on the cake.

"Having relationship problems, again," I admitted.

Nathan scoffed. "Again."

Shaking my head, I replied, "I don't need a lecture and I don't want your pity either."

"I wasn't going to give a lecture or *pity* you."

"Good. 'Cause I'm done with him."

For real this time.

He shrugged. "Cool."

"That's all you have to say?"

Nathan had seen Carlos and me arguing a few times outside of the café. One argument was so heated that Nathan felt the need to intervene. He wasn't disrespectful in his approach. However, it left a bad taste in Carlos' mouth. At that point Nathan and I hadn't known each other long, but my respect for him grew immensely that night. And after that, we quietly acknowledged the shift in our budding relationship. He'd become more protective over me. Nathan was more intentional with asking about my wellbeing. I made it clear that Carlos wasn't physically abusive, and that specific argument just went too far.

That didn't matter to Nathan. He remained consistent with checking on me. On the nights we closed together, he waited for Carlos to arrive before leaving me. And even then, he would check to see if I made it home safely.

Carlos was convinced Nathan had a crush on me. The tension between them was stifling. I never admitted that we flirted and that *I* had a tiny crush on *him* because Carlos was already insecure enough. I didn't need him bringing our drama to my job, again.

After taking another sip of his drink, he shook his head. "There's a lot I want to say, but now isn't the time."

My eyebrow rose. "What does that even mean? You're such a weirdo."

"It means, I'll wait to share my thoughts at a later date. Obviously, you're hurting right now." He cupped my chin and I swear my heart felt like it was about to explode. Just a simple touch from him set me ablaze. Standing on this roof with Nathan while being upset with Carlos was dangerous. He bit his lip, then continued, "Me saying how I feel about dude won't make you feel any better."

"Try me," I pressed.

I knew that he knew I was attracted to him. It wasn't like I tried to hide it. Flirting with him was easy and I'll admit it was fun too. However, I knew it would never go beyond that. I was so committed to Carlos that I was willing to miss out on someone far better.

Nathan laughed, then refilled our mugs.

"Zee, you're a smart woman." His eyes did a quick sweep over me. "We know there's chemistry between us. I've kept my distance because of your situation and I'm willing to give you space to get over him."

"But?"

"No, buts. I'm a patient man. Plus, I know how hard it can be to move on from someone you love. Just know, I'm here."

My lips parted and a slow breath escaped me. If only Nathan knew the ways I wanted him to be there for me. He wasn't meant to be a rebound, though. Nathan was worth way more than that.

"I don't know how much time I'll need. We were together for two years and he'd helped me through one of the roughest points in my life."

During my freshman year of college, I was on the

verge of dropping out because I didn't have enough money to cover my tuition and housing for the spring semester. Carlos and I had been dating for a few months when he offered to pay my tuition for the spring semester. I didn't question where he'd get the money from or how I'd pay him back.

Shortly after that, my dad passed away and I fell into a deep depression. My mother and I had an estranged relationship since I was a teenager. I couldn't go to her, so I leaned on Carlos for support. He was by my side through it all. Now that I'd gotten back on my feet and didn't need him as much, I realized this wasn't the healthiest situation for me.

"I understand," he said. "You ready to tell me what happened? 'Cause my thermos is running low."

"We had an argument this morning. Things got a little heated. Afterward I let him borrow my car and now he isn't answering the phone."

"Are you okay? Did he hit you?" Nathan grabbed my chin and turned my head to the side, examining my face.

"I'm fine," I told him as I removed his hand from my face.

"Where do you think he is, right now?"

"Honestly? At his baby mother's house. She was the reason we were arguing."

His eyes widened, and embarrassment washed over me. "I didn't know he had a kid."

"Two," I whispered.

He hummed. "Think he's still messing around with her?"

"I try not to think about it." I shuddered at the thought. "Just another reason why I'm done with him. Not only is he unreliable, he's not trustworthy." I sighed.

It was a slap in the face to know he went over there after every major argument. Especially if the argument was about her disrespectful ass.

"I wish I hadn't wasted so much time with him," I mumbled.

"There's a lesson you're supposed to learn from this."

I took a sip of my latte and sat the mug down. "Really? What is it?"

Nathan shrugged. "That's for you to determine. I don't know much about the dude or y'all situation to speak on it. Might sound cliche, but you deserved better." He stared at me, pensively. After a moment, I looked away as a rolling sensation shot through my stomach.

"You always know what to say."

Bringing my cup to my lips to hide my smile, I took another sip of my drink. My heart raced as we stood in silence. His eyes were glued to me as I stared straight ahead. We were a few miles out of the city and could see a few skyscrapers in the distance. I hated when he stared at me. My mind whirred with questions I was afraid of knowing the answers to.

"I hate when you do that," I said aloud.

"Do what?"

"Stare." From my peripheral, I could see a smirk Nathan reached for my waist, pulling me into him. My heart fluttered, flipped, then dropped.

"You want me to stop?" he asked against the shell of my ear.

Nathan had the nerve to smile cockily as he awaited my answer. An answer we both already knew. A chill ran through me, causing me to exhale slowly. His grip on my waist was firm and held me in place when I tried to take a step back.

"What are you thinking about?" I asked, changing the subject.

"You."

My body relaxed at his confession and my eyes met his. Those hazel orbs were fiery, confirming his words.

"I need to finish my tasks for the night," I blurted out.

"Already did them. If you're ready to leave, I can take you home."

"Yeah, today has been a lot."

Reaching for his hand, I led us to the staircase back to the café. After grabbing my bags, I met Nathan in his car. The conversation during the ride home was enough to keep my mind off my situation with Carlos. Once Nathan dropped me off, he was all I could think about. Before leaving, he promised to give me space to tie all loose ends with Carlos and I promised not to keep him waiting long.

Because truthfully, I wanted him just as much as he wanted me.

2

NATHAN

"Wassup, Mo-Mo," I said to Mocha, pinching her cheeks.

After swatting my hand, she smiled. "Nate! It's been forever." She wrapped her arms around my waist and hugged me. "I missed Natey Watey."

I smiled. "You know I *hate* when you call me that."

"And you know, I don't care. I have to be extra annoying since I haven't seen you. Feels like you've been hiding."

I didn't have the heart to tell her that I'd been avoiding this place unless it was for work.

"Yeah, it's been a minute. Who's closing with me tonight?"

A sheepish grin covered her lips. "Zee."

My heart raced at that revelation.

I nodded and kept a straight face before going to the break room to hang my coat.

Two weeks had passed since I last spoke to Zara. We agreed to keep things platonic until she spoke with her ex. I didn't think it meant she would ignore my calls and texts. After the first week, I stopped reaching out thinking it made me look too eager. Or worse, she was still with him. Her only saving grace was that she'd deleted all of their pictures from her Instagram. Which was a relief. It was hard sitting by and watching her be mistreated.

Beauty aside, Zara had a beautiful soul. She was a light that shone whenever she entered the room. She didn't know it yet, but because of her, I looked forward to coming to Milk & Honey. Even on the days when I didn't work, if I knew she was there, I stopped by. When I found out she was with someone, I was undeniably crushed.

On top of that, dude was trash and mistreated her. There were so many days she came to work looking sad or like she'd been crying. It wasn't my place to intervene, so I kept my distance. And whenever I could, I put a smile on her face.

The day I caught them arguing outside the café, I was seething. Dude really came to her place of working yelling and causing a scene cause he hadn't heard from her. My dad abused my mom, so seeing Zara and ol' boy going at it triggered something in me.

Without hesitation, I stepped in and stopped the argument. I didn't care who dude was or where he was from; he wasn't about to disrespect Zara in front of me.

From that day on, I checked on her; I watched her moods and how she interacted with us. I learned the tells from watching my mom. No matter how much make-up she wore, the sadness and defeat wore heavy on her aura. Even if the abuse wasn't physical, I could still spot a broken spirit.

When I returned from the break room, I saw Zara talking to Mocha. Zara looked different from the last time I saw her. She'd cut her hair off. Just two weeks ago, she had long dresses down her back. Now she was rocking a low cut with curls on the top. Mocha ran her hand over Zara's hair and nodded while smiling.

My chest tightened when our eyes met. Zara's eyes were red and her sienna colored skin flushed. Instead of going over there, I went back into the break room so they could continue talking. I had a few more minutes before I had to clock in. The door to the break room opened, and I looked expecting it to be Zara. I sighed when I realized it was Mocha getting her things.

Since she and Jayson finally got together, Mo had a little bounce in her walk. Whenever I brought him up, all she did was blush and giggle. I couldn't tease Jayson anymore about how bad he had it for Mocha, because the tables had turned. Now, I was over here waiting on pins and needles waiting for Zee to explain why she hadn't reached out to me.

On her way out the door, Mocha stopped and kissed me on the cheek. "Have fun working with your *boo*," she said.

I laughed. "See you later."

"Ooh! We can double date now!"

"You're getting ahead of yourself, Mo-Mo," I warned.

She waved me off. "No, I'm not. Trust me, double date coming soon."

Before I could respond, she skipped out the door.

A few minutes passed before I finally clocked in and went back to the café. Zara was at the register, taking orders while I went to the espresso machine and got to work. For most of our shift, we worked in silence. I wasn't too sure what to say to her. I half-expected an explanation for her distance, but the other part of me thought I was doing too much. Her last situation wasn't the healthiest, and she was upfront about not knowing how much time she'd need. After the evening rush passed, Zara finally broke the silence between us.

"Are we still on for tonight?" she asked. My eyebrows wrinkled as I was unsure what she was asking me. Catching wind of my confusion, she added, "After we close, we usually have coffee upstairs."

I nodded. "Yeah, we're still on."

Her lips curved into a smile that reached her brandy colored eyes. Before she walked away, I reached for her hand and said, "I like the cut."

"Thanks."

Zara ran her hand down the back of her neck as she walked away. I smiled, then returned my attention back to the espresso machine.

he next few hours flew by and before I knew it, I was filling my thermos with a brown sugar latte for Zara and me. While I finished cleaning the coffee machines and wiped down all the counters, Zara had disappeared. I figured she was already upstairs and that made me eager to finish all I had to do. The last hour was slow, so Zara got a head start on her tasks while I assisted any customers that came.

After filling the thermos, I turned off the lights in the café and headed upstairs. Zara was leaning against the wall facing me with a smile on her face. A sigh fell from my lips as I stalked over to her. Once I placed the thermos and mugs down, she pulled me into a hug. Zara buried her face into my chest as I wrapped my arms around her.

This felt right.

"I'm sorry for being so distant," she said, looking up at me. "These past weeks have been emotionally draining."

I pressed my lips onto her forehead, then said, "It's cool."

She smiled. "I knew you'd say that, and to be honest, it makes me feel even worse."

"Zee, we're good."

She stared at me a few moments more before filling our mugs. Holding the cup to her nose, she took a deep inhale then sighed.

"Brown sugar."

I nodded. "One of our favorites."

She smiled then took her first sip. "So, Carlos came over the next day."

"What happened?" I asked, my eyebrows drawing together.

"We argued." She laughed, then frowned when she noticed my scowl. "No, not like that." She paused and looked at the dark, cloudy sky. "He did his usual begging for my forgiveness spiel, and I stood my ground. After that he returned my keys, he called a friend and left."

"Have you heard from him since?"

Zara nodded, still looking at the sky. "He stopped calling for a few days. Then, he called again today."

Sitting my mug down, I looked at her through narrowed eyes.

"Today is the anniversary of my dad's passing. I thought he was calling to check on me, but it turns out, he thought today would be a good time to ask me to take him back."

My nostrils flared and hands balled into fists. "He has one more time to call you, Zee. I don't care if you don't want me involved, I'm going to step to him."

She pressed her hand into my chest. "I got it handled, Nathan. After cursing him out, I blocked him."

"Is that why you were crying earlier?"

She laughed. "It's crazy how you can always tell. I

thought I looked like my normal self by the time I got to work."

Shaking my head, I sighed.

"I can always tell."

"Yeah, 'cause you have some superpower that allows you to read people's moods?"

A half-smile rested on my lips as I contemplated whether I wanted to share how I got my *superpower*.

The look in her eyes made me comfortable with sharing my truth.

"When I was a child, my dad beat my mom and it got progressively worse over the years. She chose to stay with him until he put her in the hospital with a broken rib. No one knew what we were going through because she hid it. I didn't even know what was going on for a while. As I got older, I learned how to read her body language. Shit, I learned his, too. My mom had small tells when he beat her. There were times she looked like a zombie, just going through the motions. I realized that people are good at hiding the shit they're going through, but I've learned the eyes tell it all."

Zara's eyebrows rose and lips parted.

"Wow," she said, "I'm so sorry you went through that."

I shrugged, not knowing what to say.

"How is she now?"

With a smile, I replied, "She's doing good. After divorcing my dad, she went to therapy and eventually found love again."

"And you?" she asked with furrowed brows.

Peering down at her, I said, "I'm good, went to therapy and all that."

"Good."

"Enough about me, though. Are you good?"

She smiled. "I am and again, I'm sorry for being distant. I missed you so much."

"I missed you too, Zee."

"I want us to take things slow. Our friendship means a lot to me and I'd like to keep that same energy between us."

"You have my word that won't change."

Grabbing her chin, I kissed her lips. She smiled against my lips before wrapping her arms around my neck. Her tongue collided with mine and she moaned, pressing her body further into mine. My arms wrapped tightly around her waist holding her in place as I dropped kisses down her cheek and neck.

"Promise me one last thing," she whispered.

"What's that?"

"We'll never stop our coffee dates. I look forward to them every time we work together."

"Promise," I said, kissing her once more.

Little did she know, I looked forward to these dates too.

THE END

Thank you for taking the time to read Milk & Honey!

If you enjoyed this collection of shorts, I ask that you consider leaving a review on Amazon and/or Goodreads.

Check out the other series of short stories I have on my website.

Until next time,

D.

ACKNOWLEDGMENTS

God, for this gift!
Bria,#DRIA4L. LY.
TWC, the greater accountability partners a writer could
ask for!
Eddie, for supporting me through my long days and
nights of writing, revising, & editing!
Family and friends, for you alls unwavering
support <3

www.ingramcontent.com/pod-product-compliance
Lightning Source LLC
Chambersburg PA
CBHW031211160726
47992CB00006B/2676